THE WONDERFUL JOURNEY OF CAMERON CAT

Marjorie Newman

illustrated by

Charlotte Hard

Under this flap, and the one on page 23, you'll find lots of extra things to spot in the big pictures.

When you have finished reading the story, open out the flaps and start searching!

WALKER BOOKS

AND SUBSIDIARIES

LONDON · BOSTON · SYDNEY

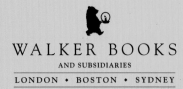

Look for these things in every big picture:

A mouse who follows Cameron wherever he goes.

Someone singing. Cameron likes to hear singing. Here is one singer. There are more.

This is the story of Cameron Cat and his wonderful journey home.

Cameron belonged to a little girl called Ann. He was curious about everything and often wandered off on his own to explore.

But one day he was a bit *too* curious, and this led to quite an adventure with lots of puzzles to solve on the way.

Can you help Cameron?

- **Read the story and solve the puzzles.**

- **Check your answers at the back when you reach the end, or if you get really stuck.**

This is Ann,
who loves her cat,
Cameron.

This is Cameron,
a rather nosy cat.

5

Cameron's adventure started one morning when he went out for a walk.

He saw a removal van parked next door, and he just had to look inside.

Please return/renew this item by the
last date shown to avoid a charge.
Books may also be renewed by phone
and Internet. May not be renewed if
required by another reader.

B A R N E T
LONDON BOROUGH

K124

Published 1998 by Walker Books Ltd
87 Vauxhall Walk, London SE11 5HJ

2 4 6 8 10 9 7 5 3

Text © 1997 Marjorie Newman
Illustrations © 1997 Charlotte Hard

This book has been typeset in
Garamond Book Educational.

Printed in Hong Kong

British Library Cataloguing in Publication Data
A catalogue record for this book is available
from the British Library.

ISBN 0-7445-4905-1 (hdbk)
ISBN 0-7445-6052-7 (pbk)

To George,
Jess, Sue, Hump
and Billy
M.N.

To Richard,
Max and Molly
C.H.

The removal men didn't see Cameron. They shut the doors and drove off! He was very excited.

Cameron had a great time climbing over the furniture in the van, but five things got broken.

 Can you find all five things and the broken pieces?

Soon the van stopped at a farm. The men began to unload. Then they went off for a cup of tea.

Cameron jumped out of the van. He just had to look around the farm before he set off for home.

But the farm animals were so startled by Cameron they ran off, and ended up in some very odd places!

Can you see them? And can you see a black cat watching?

Cameron didn't notice that the black cat was following him. He was too hungry!

Just then he saw some picnickers and made a plan. He yeowled very loudly.

Before Cameron visited the picnic ...

The plan worked! While the picnickers searched for the yeowling cat, Cameron helped himself to the picnic!

Look at the two pictures below. Can you see five changes that Cameron has made to the food and drink?

and after.

Soon Cameron came to a railway station. A train was waiting at the platform and he just had to look inside it.

But while he was exploring the whistle blew and the train moved off!

Never mind, thought Cameron and settled down on a lady's lap to enjoy the journey. To pass the time he counted sheep.

Help Cameron count the sheep. And can you tell him which two are exactly the same?

When the train stopped, Cameron got out. He saw a dark forest. He just had to go in and explore.

Deep in the forest, he heard a noise. Cameron turned and saw a pair of glowing yellow eyes.

He let out a yell and ran!

The mysterious black cat had frightened Cameron, and now he was lost.

Can you help Cameron find a route to the gate? He mustn't get his paws wet or go past foxes.

Back on the road, Cameron saw a shed. He just had to look inside.

But the gardener came and locked the door. He didn't know Cameron was in there!

Just then the black cat came round the corner. "Help!" cried Cameron. The black cat looked up shyly.

Cameron saw where the gardener had hidden the key, so he asked the black cat if she could find it.

Can you help her? The key is under the pot next to two snails, with a butterfly perched on it and a worm climbing up the side.

The black cat rescued Cameron. "Thank you!" he smiled. "But who are you?"

"I'm Jessica," she said. "I'm lonely and I have no home." "Perhaps you could live with me," said Cameron.

"I'd like that," said Jessica. They walked on together. "It's not far now!" said Cameron cheerfully.

But as they turned the corner, Cameron saw lots of his friends and relations. He just had to stop and talk. Poor Jessica lost sight of him completely.

 Can you help her find Cameron?

Back together again, the cats came to Ann's school. Cameron had always wanted to look inside.

"Let's go in and find Ann!" he cried. "I'll ask her if you can come and live with us."

Ann was very pleased to have Cameron back safely. Jessica wanted to meet Ann, but she was very shy and did not wish to be seen.

Can you find Jessica, and show her how to reach Ann on empty black tiles that touch?

Ann guessed what Cameron and Jessica wanted. "I'll ask Mum if you can live with us, Puss!" she said.

"We'll have to see what Dad thinks," said Mum. Ann knew Dad would say yes. He loved cats.

Dad did say yes, and they all had a party to celebrate. Cameron wanted his favourite plate, but Mum had forgotten where it was.

 Can you help Mum find the plate? It is yellow with a blue pattern. Now choose a plate for Jessica!

Goodbye, and thank you for making sure Cameron and his new friend came home safely.

 Look for these things in every big picture:

A fish. Cameron loves fish but he only found one on his journey. Can you spot it?

One of these flowers. Cameron always looks out for different flowers whenever he goes on an adventure.

Under this flap, and the one on page 4, you'll find lots of extra things to spot in the big pictures.

When you have finished reading the story, open out the flaps and start searching!

The Answers

- The answers to the story puzzles are shown with single black lines.

- The answers to the fun flap puzzles are shown with double black lines.

Pages 6 and 7

Pages 10 and 11

Pages 4 and 5

Pages 8 and 9

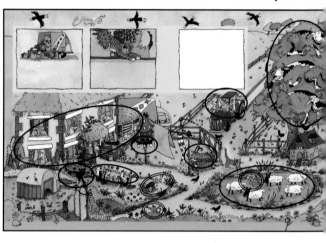

Pages 12 and 13

There are 21 sheep.

Pages 14 and 15

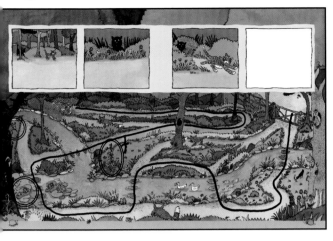

Pages 16 and 17

Pages 18 and 19

Pages 20 and 21

Pages 22 and 23

25

MORE WALKER PAPERBACKS
For You to Enjoy

Some Skill Level 1 Gamebooks

GHOST HUNT AT TREMBLY TOWERS
by Molly Williams/Chris Fisher

A hair-raising haunted-house puzzle adventure.

0-7445-6051-9   £4.99

HORNPIPE'S HUNT FOR PIRATE GOLD
by Marjorie Newman/Ben Cort

A swashbuckling pirate puzzle adventure.

0-7445-6053-5   £4.99

A BRAVE KNIGHT TO THE RESCUE!
by Stella Maidment/Cathy Gale

A thrilling knight puzzle quest.

0-7445-6055-1   £4.99

SPACE CHASE ON PLANET ZOG
by Karen King/Alan Rowe

A zappy space puzzle adventure.

0-7445-6050-0   £4.99

MYSTERY OF THE MONSTER PARTY
by Deri Robins/Anni Axworthy

A monstrous puzzle adventure.

0-7445-6054-3   £4.99

THE WONDERFUL JOURNEY OF CAMERON CAT
by Marjorie Newman/Charlotte Hard

An entertaining cat puzzle adventure.

0-7445-6052-7   £4.99

Walker Paperbacks are available from most booksellers, or by post from B.B.C.S., P.O. Box 941, Hull, North Humberside HU1 3YQ

24 hour telephone credit card line 01482 224626

To order, send: Title, author, ISBN number and price for each book ordered, your full name and address,
cheque or postal order payable to BBCS for the total amount and allow the following for postage and packing:
UK and BFPO: £1.00 for the first book, and 50p for each additional book to a maximum of £3.50.
Overseas and Eire: £2.00 for the first book, £1.00 for the second and 50p for each additional book.

Prices and availability are subject to change without notice.